100

Greatest
Quotes of
All Time

"

100

Greatest
Quotes of
All Time

"

RUPA

Published by
Rupa Publications India Pvt. Ltd 2023
7/16, Ansari Road, Daryaganj
New Delhi 110002

Sales centres:
Bengaluru Chennai
Hyderabad Jaipur Kathmandu
Kolkata Mumbai Prayagraj

P-ISBN: 978-93-5702-881-3
E-ISBN: 978-93-5702-857-8

First impression 2023

10 9 8 7 6 5 4 3 2 1

Printed in India

Contents

Introduction

'A word is dead
When it is said,
Some say.
I say it just
Begins to live
That day.'
—Emily Dickinson ('A Word is Dead')

There have been times throughout human history when words have reached greater heights than the tallest mountains, penetrated further than the deepest oceans, and shed light on the deepest recesses of our minds and hearts. At such times, the words of those who have demonstrated exceptional insight, compassion and perseverance crystallize into timeless proverbs. An astonishing trip through the history of human thought awaits you in *100 Greatest Quotes of All Time*, where these immortal words have been painstakingly compiled, organized topically and given new life.

This extraordinary anthology delves far deeper than a typical book into the human condition. Friendship, love, leadership, failure and success, teamwork, hard effort, happiness and kindness are some of the themes that run across its pages and help define human existence. Each chapter is an introspective look at the universal human experiences, hopes and beliefs that bind us together as a species.

More than just a collection of sayings, *100 Greatest Quotes of All Time* is a monument to the ability of words to motivate, direct and change people for generations to come. Each statement is like a guiding light in the maze of existence, providing direction, comfort and impetus as we try to make sense of it all.

Amidst the unvarnished realities of regular folks and the impassioned proclamations of visionary leaders can be found the sensitive sentiments of poets and the profound knowledge of ancient philosophers. These quotations speak to the depth of human connection, the tenacity of the human will, and the infinite love and compassion that lie within each of us.

Our wish is that you will be so moved by these quotations' enduring truths that you will make them your own. You will develop resilience to hardship, bravery to go after your goals, and compassion to care for your loved ones. These pages are filled with wisdom and insight that can help you in many different areas of life, whether you are looking for direction as a leader, comfort in times of despair or the drive to do something.

As you embark on your life-altering trip through the 100 greatest quotes of all time, keep in mind that you hold within your grasp the power to alter your life and the world. These words are more than just letters and numbers on a page; they represent the whole of human experience: our history, our knowledge and our promise. Let us then go off on this incredible journey together and discover the boundless opportunities that lie ahead.

On Friendship

'Lots of people want to ride with you in the limo, but what you want is someone who will take the bus with you when the limo breaks down.'

OPRAH WINFREY

'To the world you may be just one person, but to one person you may be the world.'

DR SEUSS

'I would rather walk with a friend in the dark, than alone in the light.'

HELEN KELLER

'Ultimately the bond of all companionship, whether in marriage or in friendship, is conversation.'

OSCAR WILDE

'A friend who is far away is sometimes much nearer than one who is at hand.'

KAHLIL GIBRAN

*'The only way to have a
friend is to be one.'*

RALPH WALDO EMERSON

*'Do I not destroy my enemies
when I make them my friends?'*

ABRAHAM LINCOLN

'A friend to all is a friend to none.'

ARISTOTLE

'Some people go to priests. Others to poetry. I to my friends.'

VIRGINIA WOOLF

'You can make more friends in two months by becoming interested in other people than you can in two years by trying to get other people interested in you.'

DALE CARNEGIE

'The truth is, everyone is going to hurt you. You just got to find the ones worth suffering for.'

BOB MARLEY

'Silence makes the real conversations between friends. Not the saying, but the never needing to say that counts.'

MARGARET LEE RUNBECK

On Love

'Where there is love there is life.'

MAHATMA GANDHI

'It is a curious thought, but it is only when you see people looking ridiculous that you realize just how much you love them.'

AGATHA CHRISTIE

'In love there are two things—
bodies and words.'

JOYCE CAROL OATES

*'There is always some madness in love.
But there is also always some
reason in madness.'*

FRIEDRICH NIETZSCHE

'When you realize you want to spend the rest of your life with somebody, you want the rest of your life to start as soon as possible.'

NORA EPHRON

'Never love anyone who treats you like you're ordinary.'

OSCAR WILDE

*'Love is an irresistible desire
to be irresistibly desired.'*

ROBERT FROST

*'Life is the flower for which
love is the honey.'*

VICTOR HUGO

'Love is the whole thing.
We are only pieces.'

RUMI

'Love is composed of a single soul inhabiting two bodies.'

ARISTOTLE

'Unable are the loved to die,
for love is immortality.'

EMILY DICKINSON

'Love does not consist in gazing at each other, but in looking outward together in the same direction.'

ANTOINE DE SAINT-EXUPÉRY

On Leadership

'He who has never learned to obey cannot be a good commander.'

ARISTOTLE

'The art of leadership is saying no, not saying yes. It is very easy to say yes.'

TONY BLAIR

'To lead people, walk beside them. As for the best leaders, the people do not notice their existence... When the best leader's work is done, the people say, "We did it ourselves!"'

LAO TZU

*'Innovation distinguishes between
a leader and a follower.'*

STEVE JOBS

'Don't follow the crowd,
let the crowd follow you.'

MARGARET THATCHER

'I am not afraid of an army of lions led by a sheep; I am afraid of an army of sheep led by a lion.'

ALEXANDER THE GREAT

'To do great things is difficult; but to command great things is more difficult.'

FRIEDRICH NIETZSCHE

'If you want to build a ship, don't drum up the men to gather wood, divide the work and give orders. Instead, teach them to yearn for the vast and endless sea.'

ANTOINE DE SAINT-EXUPÉRY

'Anyone can hold the helm
when the sea is calm.'

PUBLILIUS SYRUS

*'Do not follow where the path may lead.
Go instead where there is no path
and leave a trail.'*

RALPH WALDO EMERSON

'A *leader is a dealer in hope.*'

NAPOLEON BONAPARTE

'A man who wants to lead the orchestra must turn his back on the crowd.'

MAX LUCADO

'Everyone who's ever taken a shower has an idea. It's the person who gets out of the shower, dries off and does something about it who makes a difference.'

NOLAN BUSHNELL

On Failure and Success

*'I have not failed. I've just found
10,000 ways that won't work.'*

THOMAS ALVA EDISON

'Only those who dare to fail greatly can ever achieve greatly.'

ROBERT FRANCIS KENNEDY

*'We are all failures—at least the
best of us are.'*

JAMES MATTHEW BARRIE

'Failure after long perseverance is much grander than never to have a striving good enough to be called a failure.'

GEORGE ELIOT

'Fear regret more than failure.'

TARYN ROSE

'Do not judge me by my successes, judge me by how many times I fell down and got back up again.'

NELSON MANDELA

'I've missed more than 9,000 shots in my career. I've lost almost 300 games. Twenty-six times, I've been trusted to take the game winning shot and missed. I've failed over and over and over again in my life. And that is why I succeed.'

MICHAEL JORDAN

*'If you are afraid of failure, you don't
deserve to be successful.'*

CHARLES BARKLEY

'Don't fear failure—not failure, but low aim, is the crime. In great attempts it is glorious even to fail.'

BRUCE LEE

'A person who never made a mistake never tried anything new.'

ALBERT EINSTEIN

'A life spent making mistakes is not only
more honourable, but more useful than
a life spent in doing nothing.'

GEORGE BERNARD SHAW

'Success isn't overnight. It's when everyday you get a little better than the day before. It all adds up.'

DWAYNE JOHNSON

'Fortune befriends the bold.'

EMILY DICKINSON

'If you have no critics, you'll likely have no success.'

MALCOLM X

'Success usually comes to those who are too busy to be looking for it.'

HENRY DAVID THOREAU

'Success is not a good teacher, failure makes you humble.'

SHAH RUKH KHAN

'Success is not final, failure is not fatal: it is the courage to continue that counts.'

WINSTON CHURCHILL

On Teamwork

'Success is best when it's shared.'

HOWARD SCHULTZ

*'Individual honours come
with team success.'*

GILBERT ARENAS

'Alone we can do so little;
together we can do so much.'

HELEN KELLER

'Talent wins games, but teamwork and intelligence win championships.'

MICHAEL JORDAN

'If I have seen further, it is by standing on the shoulders of giants.'

ISAAC NEWTON

'It takes two flints to make a fire.'

LOUISA MAY ALCOTT

'The strength of the team is each individual member. The strength of each member is the team.'

PHIL JACKSON

*'In teamwork, silence isn't golden,
it's deadly.'*

MARK SANBORN

'Teams are incredible things. No task is too great, no accomplishment too grand, no dream too far-fetched for a team. It takes teamwork to make the dream work.'

JOHN CALVIN MAXWELL

'No one can whistle a symphony.
It takes a whole orchestra to play it.'

HALFORD EDWARD LUCCOCK

'*A successful team is a group of many hands and one mind.*'

BILL BETHEL

On Hard Work

*'The only place where success comes
before work is in the dictionary.'*

VIDAL SASSOON

'Hard work beats talent when talent doesn't work hard.'

TIM NOTKE

'I do not know anyone who has got to the top without hard work. That is the recipe. It will not always get you to the top, but should get you pretty near.'

MARGARET THATCHER

'Sometimes, you have to give up. Sometimes, knowing when to give up, when to try something else, is genius. Giving up doesn't mean stopping. Don't ever stop.'

PHIL KNIGHT

'I'm a great believer in luck, and I find the harder I work the more I have of it.'

THOMAS JEFFERSON

'Hard work is a prison sentence only if it does not have meaning. Once it does, it becomes the kind of thing that makes you grab your wife around the waist and dance a jig.'

MALCOLM GLADWELL

'Far better it is to dare mighty things, to win glorious triumphs, even though chequered by failure, than to take rank with those poor spirits who neither enjoy much nor suffer much, because they live in the grey twilight that knows neither victory nor defeat.'

THEODORE ROOSEVELT

'Without ambition one starts nothing. Without work one finishes nothing. The prize will not be sent to you. You have to win it.'

RALPH WALDO EMERSON

'The fight is won or lost far away from witnesses—behind the lines, in the gym, and out there on the road, long before I dance under those lights.'

MUHAMMAD ALI

'Do the best you can until you know better.
Then when you know better, do better.'

MAYA ANGELOU

On Happiness

'When one door of happiness closes, another opens; but often we look so long at the closed door that we do not see the one which has been opened for us.'

HELEN KELLER

*'To be stupid, selfish and have good health
are three requirements for happiness, though
if stupidity is lacking, all is lost.'*

GUSTAVE FLAUBERT

'Happiness is not the absence of problems; it's the ability to deal with them.'

STEVE MARABOLI

'Just because you are happy it does not mean that the day is perfect but that you have looked beyond its imperfections.'

BOB MARLEY

'Happiness is a gift and the trick is not to expect it, but to delight in it when it comes.'

CHARLES DICKENS

'We are all happy if we but knew it.'

FYODOR DOSTOEVSKY

'You have to be willing to get happy about nothing.'

ANDY WARHOL

'Folks are usually about as happy as they make their minds up to be.'

ABRAHAM LINCOLN

'You will never be happy if you continue to search for what happiness consists of. You will never live if you are looking for the meaning of life.'

ALBERT CAMUS

'Happiness is like those palaces in fairytales whose gates are guarded by dragons: we must fight in order to conquer it.'

ALEXANDRE DUMAS

*'The more you praise and celebrate your life,
the more there is in life to celebrate.'*

OPRAH WINFREY

'Success is getting what you want.
Happiness is wanting what you get.'

DALE CARNEGIE

*'If only we'd stop trying to be happy,
we could have a pretty good time.'*

EDITH WHARTON

On Kindness

'Be kind whenever possible.
It is always possible.'

DALAI LAMA XIV

'A part of kindness consists in loving people more than they deserve.'

JOSEPH JOUBERT

'Carry out a random act of kindness, with no expectation of reward, safe in the knowledge that one day someone might do the same for you.'

PRINCESS DIANA

'I think probably kindness is my number one attribute in a human being. I'll put it before any of the things like courage or bravery or generosity or anything else.'

ROALD DAHL

'Go and love someone exactly as they are.
And then watch how quickly they transform
into the greatest, truest version of themselves.
When one feels seen and appreciated in their
own essence, one is instantly empowered.'

WES ANGELOZZI

'Kindness is the golden chain by which society is bound together.'

JOHANN WOLFGANG VON GOETHE

'Sometimes it takes only one act of kindness and caring to change a person's life.'

JACKIE CHAN

'Be kind, for everyone you meet is fighting a hard battle.'

IAN MACLAREN

'No act of kindness, no matter how small, is ever wasted.'

AESOP

*'Be the change you wish
to see in the world.'*

MAHATMA GANDHI

'Tenderness and kindness are not signs of weakness and despair, but manifestations of strength and resolution.'

KAHLIL GIBRAN

'I honour the sanctity of all religions—
I'm not here to put them down. But the only
religion that I personally embrace
is the religion of kindness.'

LESLIE JORDAN

www.ingramcontent.com/pod-product-compliance
Lightning Source LLC
Chambersburg PA
CBHW030344030726
47499CB00003B/897